THE ABC FOR KIDS

Book of Cakes

Louise Hammond

For Georgia

Contents

As a food stylist, I am often asked to design elaborate cakes, but no project has given me more satisfaction than The ABC for Kids Book of Cakes.

Rather than relying on any complicated decorating techniques, I have used simple methods, well within the abilities of the average cook, to produce cakes which capture the fun and charm of the characters themselves.

The local supermarket lolly aisle is where you'll find your decorating needs. A big black jelly bean makes a great nose for Morgan. A marshmallow is perfect for Mr Squiggle's pom pom. And two red jelly snakes are just right for Humpty's grin. Creating the book has been great fun and I'd like to thank my assistant, Janine Gustavs, for her support.

Enjoy making the cakes and exploring ideas which the decorating techniques in this book will give you.

Louise Hammond

Louise Hammond is a Sydney based freelance food writer and stylist. She is a trained Home Economist and has an Advance Diploma from l'Ecole de Cuisine La Varenne, Paris, France.

Basic Instructions

CAKE MIXTURES

Here are two simple cake recipes, to choose from. The banana cake recipe is suitable for all the characters. The carrot cake is suitable for all the characters except Squeaky.

BANANA CAKE

125 g margarine or softened butter

1 cup brown sugar

2 eggs

2 large very ripe bananas, mashed (about 1 cup)

1½ cups self-raising flour

1 teaspoon cinnamon

Method

Beat margarine or butter and brown sugar together until creamy. Add eggs one at a time, beating well between each addition. Using a wooden spoon, beat in mashed banana. Do not be concerned if mixture appears to curdle. Sift flour and cinnamon together and fold into the mixture. Pour into prepared pan and bake at 180°C until firm, as advised in recipe for the character you are making.

CARROT CAKE

125 g margarine or softened butter

½ cup caster sugar

½ teaspoon finely grated orange zest

2 eggs

1½ cups grated carrot

1¾ cups self-raising flour

1 teaspoon cinnamon

2 tablespoons freshly squeezed orange juice

Method

Beat margarine or butter, caster sugar and orange zest together until creamy.

Add eggs, one at a time, beating well between each addition. Using a wooden spoon stir in grated carrot. Do not be concerned if mixture appears to curdle. Sift flour and cinnamon together and fold into the mixture, alternating with orange juice. Pour into prepared pan and bake at 170°C until firm, as advised in recipe for the character you are making.

Notes

- When pouring cake mixture into prepared pan, always use a spatula to spread mixture evenly. This will minimise uneven rising.

- A 340 g packet butter cake mix can be used as a substitute for the above recipes.

- Packet mix is too moist to bake in a nut roll tin and is unsuitable for the Rocket Clock.

- Where the recipe calls for 2 quantities of cake mixture, simply double the ingredients and use a large mixing bowl.

- Cakes baked the day before are easier to cut. The banana cake and carrot cake will keep fresh for up to four days. Packet cakes will begin to go stale after a day or two.

- Store cakes in an airtight container lined with non-stick baking paper. Alternatively, place on a cake board, covered with a sheet of non-stick baking paper. Cover loosely with plastic wrap and store in a cool place.

- Let cake rest in pan for ten minutes after baking before turning out onto a wire rack to cool.

- Slip a piece of thick cardboard under the cold cake when transferring from wire rack to cutting board or cake board. Gently remove cardboard from under cake.

BISCUIT DOUGH

Large Quantity

175 g margarine or softened butter

¾ cup caster sugar

¼ teaspoon vanilla essence

1 egg and 1 egg yolk, lightly beaten

3 cups plain flour

1½ teaspoons bicarbonate of soda

Small Quantity

75 g margarine or softened butter

⅓ cup caster sugar

⅛ teaspoon vanilla essence

1 egg, lightly beaten

1¼ cups plain flour

½ teaspoon bicarbonate of soda

Method

Beat margarine or butter and caster sugar together until creamy. Add vanilla and egg. Beat well. Sift flour and bicarbonate of soda together and stir into the mixture to form a firm dough. Add a little cold water if dough is too dry. Refrigerate for one hour. Roll out between two sheets of non-stick baking paper to the desired thickness or shape.

BAKING PANS

1   Nut roll tin

2   23 cm square slab pan

3   25 cm x 30 cm lamington pan

4   10 cup capacity Dolly Varden cake pan

5   9 cup capacity aluminium pudding steamer

6   Deep 20 cm round cake pan

7   17 cm round cake pan

A variety of standard cake pans are used in the following recipes. They can be obtained from most large department stores, cookware shops or supermarkets. The Dolly Varden cake pan can be obtained from some large department stores, specialty cookware shops or cake decoration suppliers.

Basic Instructions

Pan Preparation

Non-stick cooking spray was used to grease bakeware. Where lining was required, non-stick baking paper was used on pan base.

Baking Times

Baking times will vary. You will find a guide to baking times with the instructions for making each cake. However, it is best to test the cake by inserting a fine wooden skewer in the centre. If it comes out clean, the cake is cooked.

If using a fan forced oven reduce the temperature stated in the recipe by 10°C. Fan forced ovens also produce an even heat, allowing two cakes to be baked at one time. When baking two cakes together in a conventional oven, use separate shelves and swap the cakes' positions about halfway through the baking time.

FROSTING & ICINGS

FROSTING

This simple frosting is used on all the cakes. It spreads smoothly, stays creamy, and does not set to a crust.

200 g spreadable margarine (not cooking margarine)

1½ cups sifted pure icing sugar

1 teaspoon vanilla essence

Method

Using an electric mixer on medium speed, beat ingredients together until light (about 4 minutes).

ROYAL ICING

Royal icing sets firm. It is used to stick cakes together and for some decorative details.

1 egg white

1¼ to 1¾ cups sifted pure icing sugar

Method

Beat egg white for about 5 seconds. Gradually beat in enough icing sugar to form a stiff but spreadable consistency.

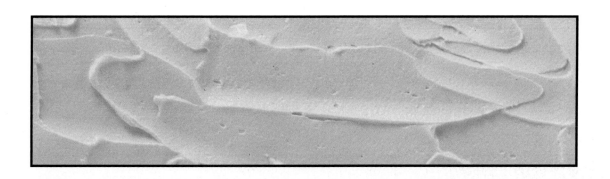

SOFT ICING

Soft icing is pliable and can be bought, usually from the sugar section, of most supermarkets. It is necessary to knead it to a smooth consistency, particularly in cold weather. Dust hands with sifted pure icing sugar to stop icing from becoming too sticky. In warm weather or when adding food colouring, extra icing sugar may be needed.

Colouring Soft Icing

Knead the icing to a smooth consistency. Make a depression with your thumb. Place a few drops of food colouring in the depression and continue kneading until the colour is evenly distributed. Add more colouring if necessary.

Note: Food colouring on hands will wash off.

Rolling Soft Icing

Place kneaded soft icing between two sheets of non-stick baking paper. Roll out as stated in the recipe. Leave icing between paper if it requires refrigeration. Remove top layer of paper before cutting to shape.

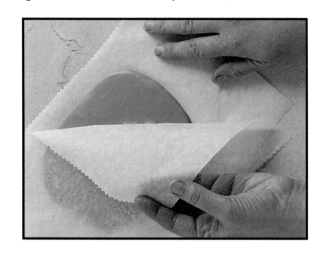

Notes

- Frost or ice cakes with the smooth underside facing up.
- Banana cake and carrot cake usually rise evenly. Packet cakes, however, tend to rise to a peak and may need levelling if the peak is pronounced.
- Cakes can be iced and decorated the day before. Store, uncovered, in a cool place (not refrigerator), away from direct sunlight. Any fabric bows should be added on the day.

FOOD COLOURINGS

Food colourings can be bought in three forms: powder, paste and liquid. Powders and pastes give a more intense colour than liquids. Powders should be dissolved with a small amount of hot water before use. Pastes and liquids can be added directly to frostings and icings. Always add a small amount at first, then gradually add more until the desired colour is achieved. Food colourings are available from cake decoration suppliers and some health food stores.

Note: Parisian essence can be used instead of caramel food colouring to give a similar colour.

DECORATIONS

'HAPPY BIRTHDAY' BANNER

YOU WILL NEED

50 g pre-packaged white soft icing

sifted pure icing sugar

1 Cruskit biscuit

1 candy fruit stick

1 plastic 'Happy Birthday' sign (available from cake decoration suppliers and most cake shops)

Method

Knead icing with a little pure icing sugar. Roll out between two sheets of non-stick baking paper to a rectangular shape, slightly larger than the Cruskit. Place Cruskit firmly on top of the icing as shown in **Step 1**. Cut icing to shape of Cruskit and remove off-cuts. Turn over and peel off paper. Cut candy fruit stick into thin slices. Lightly moisten back of each slice before pressing onto icing to form border as shown in **Step 2**. Gently press the plastic 'Happy Birthday' sign into position as shown in **Step 3**.

STEP **2**

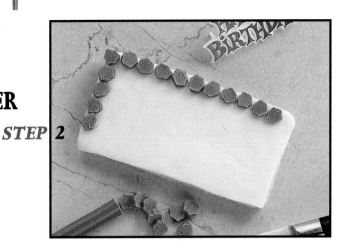

STEP **3**

GIFT BOX PLAQUE

YOU WILL NEED

1 Cruskit biscuit

1 teaspoon margarine

hundreds and thousands

1 candy fruit stick or musk stick

Method

Spread Cruskit with margarine, sprinkle with hundreds and thousands and place on cake. Cut candy fruit stick in half lengthwise. Trim one half for ribbon and cut other half into five triangles for bow. Arrange as shown in picture.

STEP **1**

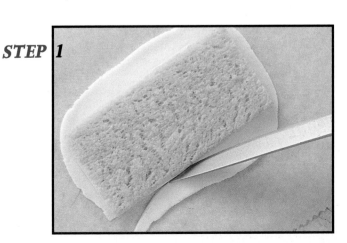

9

BANDAIDS

YOU WILL NEED

50 g pre-packaged white soft icing

sifted pure icing sugar

caramel food colouring

1 real bandaid for template

Method

Knead icing with a little pure icing sugar.
Colour beige using caramel food colouring. Roll
out between two sheets of non-stick baking
paper to a rectangular shape approximately
9 cm x 6 cm. Refrigerate 30 minutes.

Place bandaid on top of icing and cut to
shape as shown in **Step 1**. Repeat to make
another bandaid shape. Form pad creases with
back of knife as shown in **Step 2**. Make holes
with a fork as shown in **Step 3**.

STEP 1

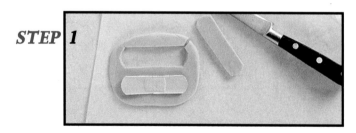

STEP 2

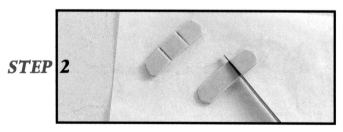

STEP 3

CLOCK FACE NUMBERS

Using a skewer, prick holes in the clock face to
form numbers. Place a blue hundred and
thousand in each hole.
Push down with the tip
of the skewer.

CAKE BOARDS

The size of the cake board required is indicated
in each recipe, however a chopping board or
platter of a similar size may be used.

Cake boards can be made from MDF
(medium density fibreboard) obtainable from
most hardware stores. Cover boards with white
self-adhesive vinyl. Cake boards covered with
silver or gold paper are available from cake
decoration suppliers.

Covering Round Cake Boards

Place board on a sheet of self-adhesive vinyl.
Cut vinyl in a circle 5 cm larger than the board.
Carefully trace around outline of board with a
sharp knife to penetrate backing paper. Cut the
vinyl at 5 cm intervals around the circle and
peel off paper. Fold
sticky vinyl around
board as shown in
photograph.

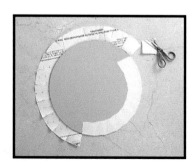

FOOD SENSITIVITIES AND ALLERGIES

Some children are sensitive or allergic to certain foods. To help overcome this problem we have tested alternatives to certain ingredients used in the recipes.

Food Colourings

Yellow Mix powdered turmeric with a little hot water to form a paste.

Pink The juice of canned beetroot will give a pale pink.

Raspberry pink Cook fresh or frozen raspberries over a gentle heat, stirring often, until very thick. Sieve mixture to remove pulp. Allow to cool. The colour will be slightly less bright.

Violet Cook fresh or frozen blueberries over a gentle heat, stirring often, until very thick. Sieve mixture to remove pulp. Allow to cool.

Green Fresh spinach juice will give a pale green. (Remove stalks before juicing.)

Caramel Use a parisian essence which is made from natural caramel, or use light carob powder for frosting.

Cocoa powder Although cocoa powder is a natural substance, some children have a sensitivity to it. Substitute dark carob powder for cocoa.

Notes

- Do not add large amounts of these liquids to the frosting or it will curdle. Excessive liquid added to the soft icing will make it sticky.
- Commercial sweets often contain food colourings. Simply remove these sweets from the cake before serving to the child. The same can be done for any coloured soft icing.
- Humpty's frosting contains no food colouring.
- Jemima and Bananas in Pyjamas have large areas of uncoloured frosting.

Gluten Intolerance

'Healtheries Gluten Free Baking and Bread Mix' can be substituted for self-raising flour in both the banana cake and carrot cake recipes.

Milk Allergy

'Sundew Milk Free Margarine' can be used in the banana cake, the carrot cake, the biscuit recipes and the frosting.

Egg Allergy

'Country Harvest Egg Replacer Powder' made to the directions on the packet can be substituted for eggs in both the banana cake and the carrot cake recipes.

11

Humpty

2 quantities cake mixture
(see recipes page 5)

1½ quantities frosting (see recipe page 7)

green and white liquorice allsorts for *collar*

1 white marshmallow for *eyes*

3 liquorice sticks for *eyes, eyebrows and hair*

red Smarties for *polkadots*

1 large white marshmallow for *nose*

2 red jelly snakes for *mouth*

4 pre-packaged Savoiardi biscuits for *arms and legs*

red satin ribbon for *bow*

To bake

Pour cake mixture equally into two 10 cup capacity greased Dolly Varden cake pans. Place side by side on a baking tray for stability and bake at the temperature stated in recipe until firm, about 1 hr - 1 hr 15 minutes.

To assemble

Cut a 2 cm thick slice from the narrow end of one cake as shown in **Step 1**. Invert cut cake and secure to 30 cm round cake board with 1 teaspoon frosting. Spread top of cake with ½ cup frosting and place other cake on top as shown in **Step 2**. Cover entire cake with remaining frosting.

To decorate

Slice green liquorice allsorts into thin squares and place side by side around Humpty's neck to form a green collar band. Repeat with squares of white liquorice allsorts to form another band underneath, leaving a small gap either side of the cake for arms.

Cut two slices of marshmallow and place in eye positions, sticky sides facing out. Top each with a slice of liquorice stick. Cut thin slices of liquorice stick and use for eyebrows. Use red Smarties for polkadots, large marshmallow for nose, snakes for mouth, and thin strips of remaining liquorice sticks for hair.

Trim one end of each Savoiardi biscuit, using a gentle sawing action. Cut a small 'v' in each arm to indicate thumbs. Place into arm and leg positions as shown in **Step 3**.

STEP 3

STEP 1

STEP 2

The young helper can . . .

- Place bow on collar.

Notes

- Should you only have one 10 cup capacity Dolly Varden cake pan, prepare and bake the cakes one at a time.
- Non-stick cooking spray gives the best results when greasing Dolly Varden cake pans.

Jemima

Jemima

YOU WILL NEED

2 quantities cake mixture (see recipe page 5)

1½ quantities frosting (see recipe page 7)

blue and black food colourings

2 tablespoons cocoa powder, sifted

yellow candy fruit sticks for *overalls*

liquorice bullets for *hair*

1 pink marshmallow for *cheeks*

Smarties for *eyes, shirt polkadots and buttons*

red jelly snake for *mouth*

2 pre-packaged Savoiardi biscuits for *arms*

thin blue ribbon for *two bows*

To bake

Pour 2 cups cake mixture into a greased and lined 17 cm round cake pan. Pour remaining cake mixture into a similarly prepared 25 cm x 30 cm lamington pan. Bake at temperature stated in recipe until firm. Round cake will take about 30-35 minutes, rectangular cake will take about 35-45 minutes.

Jemima

To assemble

Cut Jemima's templates (see page 75) and pin to cakes as shown in **Step 1**. Cut to shape.

Use remainder of cake to cut out legs, shoes and pigtail shapes.

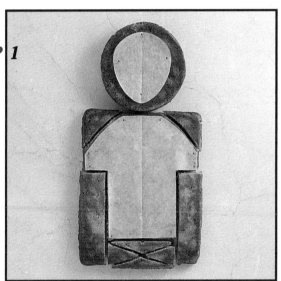

STEP 1

Arrange body, head and legs on a 30 cm x 60 cm cake board, leaving pigtails and shoes aside as shown in **Step 2**.

To decorate

Colour ½ cup frosting blue. Mix sifted cocoa into ½ cup frosting. Colour ¼ cup frosting dark grey. Leave remaining frosting uncoloured.

As shown in **Step 3**, spread blue frosting over upper body and sleeves. Spread uncoloured frosting over face, lower body and legs. Spread cocoa coloured frosting around head for hair, and over pigtails. Spread dark grey frosting over shoes. Place pigtails and shoes into position.

Cut candy fruit sticks in half lengthwise and lay in position to form overalls. Place liquorice bullets on hair and pigtails. Cut two slices of pink marshmallow and position on face for cheeks. Use two dark brown Smarties for eyes and a sliver of red snake for mouth. Trim Savoiardi biscuits to 9 cm lengths, using a gentle sawing action. Cut a small 'v' in each biscuit to indicate thumbs. Place into position as shown in final picture.

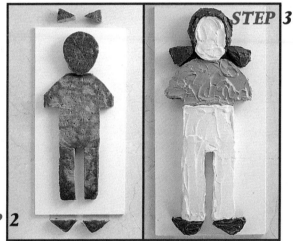

STEP 2 **STEP 3**

The young helper can . . .

- Place Smarties on shirt for polkadots and position two blue Smarties for overall buttons.
- Position blue bows on pigtails.

Notes

- *Use a warm, dry metal spatula to spread cocoa frosting.*
- *Musk sticks or a variety of coloured candy fruit sticks can be used for overalls.*

Flower Clock

YOU WILL NEED

1 large quantity biscuit dough
(see recipe page 6)

1 quantity cake mixture (see recipes page 5)

125 g pre-packaged white soft icing

yellow, raspberry pink and violet food colourings

hundreds and thousands for numbers

1½ quantities frosting (see recipe page 7)

liquorice stick for clock hands

2 Liquorice Rainbow Twists for stem

To bake

Roll ⅔ biscuit dough into a circular shape, slightly larger than 27 cm (see directions for rolling biscuit dough with recipe page 6). Cut Flower Clock base template (see page 75) and place template on top of rolled dough. Cut dough to shape of template and remove dough off-cuts. Cut out eight small 'v's at equal distances apart around rim of cirlce as shown in **Step 1**.

STEP 1

Lift paper base with rolled biscuit dough onto a baking tray. Set aside.

Roll out remaining biscuit dough to 5 mm thickness. Cut with a flower shaped cookie cutter. Place flower biscuits on a baking tray lined with non-stick baking paper. Bake flower biscuits and Flower Clock biscuit base at 170°C until golden brown. Flower biscuits will take about 25-35 minutes. Biscuit base will take about 35-45 minuites.

Pour cake mixture into a greased and lined deep 20 cm round cake pan. Bake at temperature stated in recipe until firm, about 35-45 minutes.

To decorate

Colour white soft icing yellow. Wrap 25 g (about the size of a walnut) in plastic wrap and set aside. Roll remainder to a circle slightly larger than 11 cm (see directions for rolling icing page 8). Cut Flower Clock face template (see page 75) and place onto rolled icing. Cut icing to shape and remove off-cuts. As shown in **Step 2**, form a pattern around edge of circle using a small metal screw cap for cutter (we used the cap from a vanilla essence bottle). Mark numbers on clock face using blue hundreds and thousands (see directions page 10). Refrigerate uncovered until required.

Flower Clock

Colour half of frosting raspberry pink. Colour remaining frosting violet. Reserve 2 tablespoons of each colour frosting for flower biscuits. Spread remaining raspberry pink frosting over biscuit base.

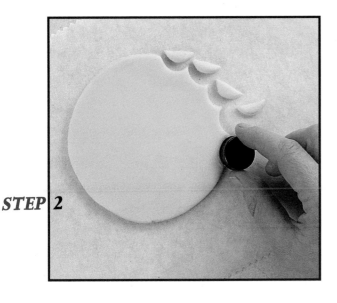

STEP 2

Level cake if necessary. Cut out eight small 'v's at equal distances apart around rim of cake. Cover cake with violet frosting.

Spread flower biscuits with reserved raspberry pink and violet frosting. Form small balls (about size of unshelled hazelnuts) from remaining yellow soft icing. Slightly flatten balls and place onto each biscuit.

To assemble

Position frosted biscuit base on 30cm x 60 cm cake board. Place frosted cake on top of base. Carefully lift clock face off paper and place into position. Place fine strips of liquorice on clock face for hands.

The young helper can . . .

- Position Liquorice Rainbow Twists for stem.
- Place flower biscuits around stem.

Notes

- Biscuit base and flower biscuits can be made up to a week in advance and stored in an airtight container.
- Plain liquorice twists may be used for stem.

Slush

YOU WILL NEED

2 quantities of cake mixture
(see recipes page 5)

2 quantities of royal icing
(see recipe page 7)

1 small box for trough

candy coated popcorn to fill trough

1 x 250 g pre-packaged Swiss roll for *head*

1 small ice cream cone for *ears*

4 pre-packaged jam fairy cakes for *hooves*

1½ quantities frosting
(see recipe page 7)

raspberry pink food colouring

1 liquorice allsort for *eyes and nostrils*

brown Smarties and brown Vice Versas for *spots*

3 long wooden skewers, cut into 12 cm lengths

toothpicks

1 pink pipe cleaner for *tail*

Slush

To bake

Pour cake mixture equally into two greased 9 cup capacity aluminium pudding steamers. Bake at the temperature stated in recipe until firm, about 1 hour-1 hour 10 minutes.

To assemble

Level cakes, if necessary, and sandwich together with half of the royal icing. Secure with two wooden skewers as shown in **Step 1**. Cut a 3 cm thick vertical slice from the joined cakes as shown in **Step 2**. Use 2 tablespoons royal icing to secure cake (cut side down) to a 25 cm x 45 cm cakeboard.

***STEP* 2**

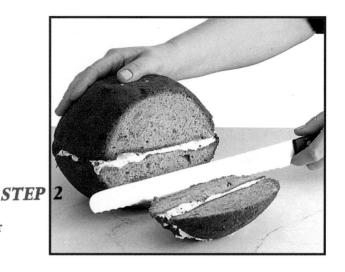

***STEP* 3**

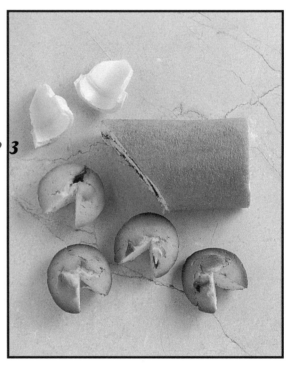

***STEP* 1**

As shown in **Step 3**, cut Swiss roll to 13cm length, then trim at an angle so it will sit flush to cake when set into head position. Cut ice cream cone in half vertically and trim to ear shapes. Cut a 'v' in each fairy cake to form hooves. Spread 1 tablespoon royal icing on base of trough and secure to cake board 8 cm from Slush's body. Fill trough with popcorn.

Slush

As shown in **Step 4**, spread 2 tablespoons royal icing on cake where snout will be attached.

STEP 4

Colour frosting raspberry pink. Spread snout end of Slush's head with some of the pink frosting. Rest snout on trough and secure other end of Swiss roll to royal icing on body, using remaining wooden skewer. Spread bottom end of ears with a little royal icing and secure in position with toothpicks as shown in **Step 5**.

STEP 5

To decorate

Cover cake with pink frosting then, one at a time, cover hooves with frosting and position against body. Slice white part off liquorice allsort. Cut into two small circles for eyes. Press a tiny piece of liquorice (from liquorice allsort) onto each eye and place on cake. Cut two small pieces of liquorice for nostrils. Curl pipe cleaner and insert into cake for tail.

The young helper can . . .

- Place brown Smarties and brown Vice Versas on body for spots.

Notes

- Should you only have one 9 cup capacity pudding steamer, prepare and bake the cakes one at a time.
- Non-stick cooking spray gives the best results for greasing pudding steamer.
- Be aware of the skewers and toothpicks when serving cake.

Diddle

YOU WILL NEED

1 quantity cake mixture (see recipes page 5)

1 quantity frosting (see recipe page 7)

black food colouring

2 pre-packaged jam fairy cakes for head

100 g white soft icing for chest and paws

3 liquorice sticks
for paw trim, ears, whiskers and tail

6 small pre-packaged Savoiardi-style
sponge finger biscuits for legs

1 yellow liquorice allsort for eyes

green candy fruit stick for ribbon and bow

1 toothpick, cut to 5 cm length

1 wooden skewer, cut to 13 cm length

Diddle

To bake

Pour cake mixture into a greased 10 cup capacity Dolly Varden cake pan. Place on a baking tray for stability and bake at temperature stated in recipe until firm, about 1 hr - 1 hr 15 minutes.

To assemble

Trim cake to a more tapered shape as shown in **Step 1**.

STEP 2

STEP 1

Colour frosting dark grey. Level tops of fairy cakes. Sandwich together with a little frosting and secure with toothpick. Cut a small slice off one side to form head as shown in **Step 2**.

Use a little frosting to secure Diddle's body to centre of a 25 cm round cake board. Secure head to body using skewer as shown in **Step 3**.

STEP 3

To decorate

Cover head and body with dark grey frosting. Roll out white soft icing into a circle, 5 mm thick (see directions for rolling icing page 8). Refrigerate 30 minutes. Cut Diddle's chest and paw templates (see page 78). Place chest template on icing. Cut to shape and place white chest into position on cake. Use paw template to cut four paws from remaining icing. Set paws aside.

Cut two biscuits to 7 cm length, cover one with frosting and place into thigh position as shown in **Step 4**. Repeat with other cut biscuit on other side of cake.

One at a time, cover remaining biscuits with frosting and set into leg positions. Gently press thin strips of liquorice onto paws and place at end of each leg.

Cut ear shapes from liquorice stick and place into position. Slice yellow part off liquorice allsort and cut to shape for eyes. Press a sliver of the liquorice onto each eye and place into positions. Place thin strips of liquorice onto face for whiskers.

Cut green candy fruit stick in half lengthwise and cut a long thin strip from one half to form a ribbon. Place around neck. Cut a bow shape from other half of candy fruit stick and position on cake as shown in final picture.

The young helper can . . .

- Help join two liquorice sticks together for Diddle's tail.

STEP 4

Notes

- Non-stick cooking spray gives the best result for greasing Dolly Varden cake pan.
- Be aware of toothpick and skewer when serving cake.

Rocket Clock

YOU WILL NEED

1 small quantity biscuit dough
(see recipe page 6)

2 quantities cake mixture
(see recipes page 5)

1 quantity royal icing
(see recipe page 7)

2 Cruskit biscuits for fins

candy fruit sticks for nose cone and fins

440 g pre-packaged white soft icing

yellow, green, violet and blue food colourings

1 Granita biscuit for back of clock face

hundreds and thousands for numbers

liquorice stick for hands on clock face

1 egg white, lightly beaten

1½ quantities frosting
(see recipe page 7)

silver cachous

1 x 20 cm long wooden skewer

1 toothpick

Note

● This cake takes longer to assemble and decorate than the other cakes. It is recommended that the star biscuits be baked up to a week in advance and stored in an airtight container.

Rocket Clock

To bake

Roll biscuit dough to 5 mm thickness (see directions for rolling biscuit dough with recipe page 6). Cut with a star shaped cookie cutter. Place star biscuits on a baking tray lined with non-stick baking paper and bake at 170°C for 25-30 minutes, until golden brown.

Pour 1½ cups cake mixture into a greased nut roll tin, place on a baking tray. Pour remaining mixture into a greased 10 cup capacity Dolly Varden cake pan and place on same baking tray. Bake at temperature stated in recipe until firm. Cylindrical cake, about 30-35 minutes. Dolly Varden cake, 1 hr 10 minutes - 1 hr 20 minutes.

To assemble

Level cakes, if necessary. Spread 2 tablespoons royal icing over the broad end of Dolly Varden cake, invert and secure to a 30 cm round cake board. Spread top of Dolly Varden cake with 1 tablespoon royal icing and place cylindrical cake on top. Secure with long wooden skewer as shown in **Step 1**. Spread 1 tablespoon royal icing around cake join.

STEP 1

To decorate

Cut seven candy fruit sticks in half lengthwise. Cut fin template (see page 75). Place on a Cruskit and cut to shape. Repeat with second Cruskit. Thinly spread one side of each Cruskit fin (the side which will face forward) with royal icing. Trim candy fruit stick halves and align on iced side of each Cruskit fin, leaving a 1 cm gap down each inner edge as shown in **Step 2**.

STEP 2

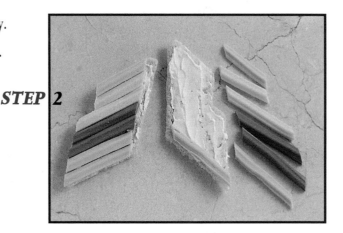

STEP 3

Cut a 1 cm deep groove the length of the fins down each side of the cake. Spread a little royal icing along the inner edge of each fin and gently ease into the corresponding grooves as shown in **Step 3**.

STEP 4

STEP 6

Form 100g white soft icing into a 5 cm high cone shape and thinly cover with royal icing. Cut six candy fruit sticks in half lengthwise. Place on a baking tray lined with non-stick baking paper and bake at 180°C for 20-30 seconds, until pliable. Wrap sticks around cone as shown in **Step 4**.

Set nose cone aside.

Colour 140 g white soft icing yellow. Wrap 100 g in plastic wrap and set aside. Roll out remaining yellow icing to an 8 cm diameter circle (see directions for rolling soft icing page 8). Gently press Granita biscuit onto icing circle and cut to shape to form clock face as shown in **Step 5**. Turn over and peel away paper. Mark numbers on clock face using blue hundreds and thousands (see directions page 10). Cut strips of liquorice for clock hands, gently press on face and set aside.

Colour 100 g white soft icing green and colour 100 g violet. Roll out green, violet and reserved yellow icing to 5 mm thickness. Refrigerate for 30 minutes. Cut coloured icings with the star shaped cookie cutter. Reserve four icing stars for decoration and refrigerate until needed. Lightly brush star biscuits with egg white. Top each biscuit with a coloured icing star as shown in **Step 6**.

Colour frosting blue and spread over cake, leaving fins exposed. With a small spatula or butterknife make ridges down lower section of the rocket. Gently ease toothpick through centre of clock face and secure to upper section of rocket. Top cake with reserved nose cone and decorate with the four reserved icing stars. Place silver cachous on cake using tweezers.

The young helper can . . .

- Place iced star biscuits around cake.

Notes

- Non-stick cooking spray gives the best result for greasing both the nut roll tin and the Dolly Varden cake pan.
- Be aware of skewer and toothpick when serving cake.

STEP 5

33

Bananas in Pyjamas

YOU WILL NEED

2 quantities of cake mixture
(see recipes page 5)

1½ quantities frosting
(see recipe page 7)

yellow and blue food colourings

250 g pre-packaged white soft icing

'Happy Birthday' banner
(see page 9)

1 chocolate coated liquorice stick for stem

liquorice stick for mouth and eyes

3 small white round sherbet sweets for buttons

Bananas in Pyjamas

To bake

Pour cake mixture into two greased and lined 23 cm square slab pans. Bake at temperature stated in recipe until firm, about 25-35 minutes.

To assemble

Cut Bananas in Pyjamas template (see page 72) and pin to cakes. Cut to shape as shown in **Step 1**. Using a 6 cm round cutter, cut a semicircle from remaining cake. Split semicircle in halves horizontally to form two hands. Cut two small 'v's in each to form fingers. Place Bananas in Pyjamas cakes on a 30 cm x 60 cm cake board as shown in **Step 2**, leaving hands aside.

To decorate

Colour ⅓ of the frosting yellow and spread over head and hands. Spread remaining uncoloured frosting over Banana's body as shown in **Step 3**.

STEP 1

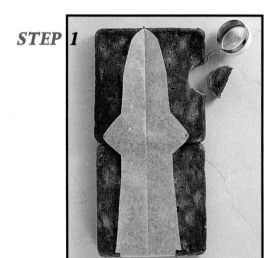

STEP 3

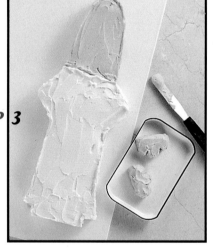

STEP 2

Wrap a pea size piece of white soft icing in plastic wrap and set aside for making centres of 'B' and whites of eyes. Roll out 100 g of white soft icing to a rectangular shape 9 cm x 11 cm (see directions for rolling icing page 8) and refrigerate until required. Colour remaining icing blue and roll into a rectangular shape 12 cm x 13 cm, about 5 mm thick. Refrigerate one hour. Trim edges of blue rectangle and cut into thirteen 1 cm wide strips as shown in **Step 4**.

36

STEP 4

Cut 1 cm off two of the strips for sleeves. Keep off-cuts. Arrange strips on cake as shown in **Step 5**.

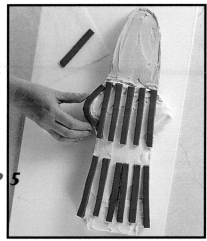

STEP 5

Gently bend sleeve strips and fit into place. Roll some of the blue icing off-cuts into a small ball. Flatten, cut in half and use for inner sleeves. Cut 'B1' or 'B2' from remaining off-cuts and fill centre of the 'B' with two very small flattened balls of reserved white soft icing.

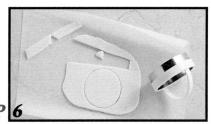

STEP 6

As shown in **Step 6**, cut collar template (see page 73) and place on rolled out white soft icing. Cut to shape and put in place. Decorate with insignia. Cut a 6 cm circle from remaining rolled out white soft icing. Cut in half and place on cake to form shoes. Set 'Happy Birthday' banner on Bananas in Pyjamas' waist and place a hand on each side. Cut an 8 cm length of chocolate coated liquorice stick and trim cut end into a point. Make an incision in the top of the head and insert the chocolate coated liquorice stick. Cut liquorice stick into eye and mouth shapes. Highlight each eye with a very small flattened ball of the reserved white soft icing.

The young helper can . . .

- Place the liquorice eyes and mouth on Bananas in Pyjamas' face and position the round white sherbet sweet buttons on his jacket.

Notes

- Should you only have one 23 cm square slab pan, prepare and bake the cakes one at a time.

- A 6 cm round template (see page 75) can be used instead of cutter.

- Gift box plaque (see page 9) may be used instead of the 'Happy Birthday' banner.

Lulu

YOU WILL NEED

2 quantities cake mixture
(see recipes page 5)

1½ quantities frosting
(see recipe page 7)

½ cup cocoa powder, sifted

raspberry pink and green food colourings

musk sticks for *shoes and collar*

7 lime candy fruit sticks for *dress trim*

liquorice stick for *mouth*

2 milk bottle sweets for *hair bow*

gift box plaque
(see page 9)

2 dark brown Smarties for *eyes*

1 large black jelly bean for *nose*

1 green liquorice allsort for *dress button*

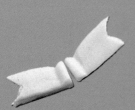

Lulu

To bake

Pour 2 cups cake mixture into a greased and lined 17 cm round cake pan. Pour remaining cake mixture into a similarly prepared 25 cm x 30 cm lamington pan. Bake at temperature stated in recipe until firm. Round cake will take about 30-35 minutes, rectangular cake will take about 35-45 minutes.

To assemble

Cut Lulu's body template (see page 74) and Teddy's head template (see page 75) and pin to cakes as shown in **Step 1**.

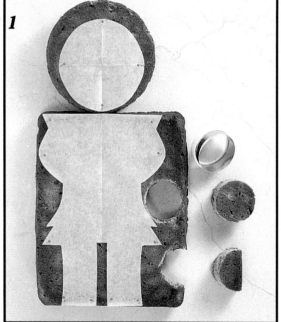

STEP **1**

Cut to shape. Using a 6 cm round cutter, cut a circle and semicircle from remaining rectangular cake. Trim circle to a dome shape for snout. Split semicircle in halves horizontally

to form two hands and cut two small 'v's in each to indicate fingers. Using the same 6 cm round cutter, cut two ear shapes from remaining round cake as shown in **Step 2**. Scoop out a small hollow in each.

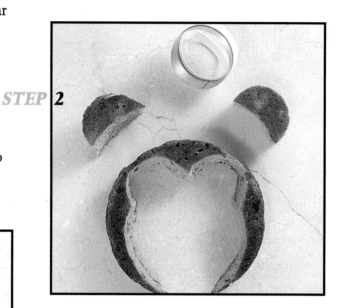

STEP **2**

Place Lulu on a 30 cm x 60 cm cake board as shown in **Step 3**, leaving hands aside.

STEP **3**

To decorate

Blend cocoa into half the frosting. Colour half the remaining frosting raspberry pink and the remainder green. Spread frosting over cake as shown in **Step 4**.

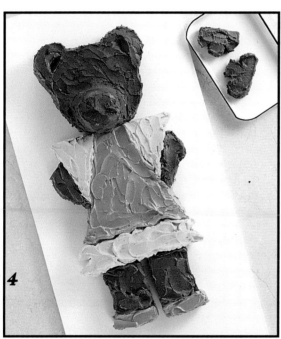

STEP **4**

Trim musk sticks and use to make shoe soles, straps and dress collar. Place lime candy fruit sticks on a baking tray lined with non-stick baking paper and bake at 180°C for 20-30 seconds, until pliable. Gently bend into waves, and when cool use to decorate Lulu's dress. Place trimmed milk bottles on Lulu's head for bows and use the trimmed liquorice for mouth. Set gift box plaque at Lulu's waist and place a hand on each side, as shown in final picture.

The young helper can . . .

- Position the Smarties on Lulu's face for eyes, the large black jelly bean for nose, and a slice of green liquorice allsort on dress for button.

Notes

- *A 6cm round template (see page 75) can be used instead of cutter.*

- *Use a warm, dry, metal spatula to spread cocoa frosting.*

- *'Happy Birthday' banner (see page 9) may be used instead of the gift box plaque.*

- *A small chocolate egg may be used instead of the large black jelly bean for Lulu's nose.*

Morgan

YOU WILL NEED

2 quantities cake mixture
(see recipes page 5)

1½ quantities frosting
(see recipe page 7)

caramel, orange, violet and green
food colourings

90 g pre-packaged white soft icing

4 lime milk bottle sweets
for *shoe bows*

2 large round peppermints
for *shoe tongues*

2 lime candy fruit sticks
for *shoelaces and collar*

'Happy Birthday' banner
(see page 9)

musk sticks for 'M's

liquorice stick for *mouth*

2 dark brown Smarties for *eyes*

1 large black jelly bean for *nose*

To bake

Pour 2 cups cake mixture into a greased and lined 17 cm round cake pan. Pour remaining cake mixture into a similarly prepared 25 cm x 30 cm lamington pan. Bake at temperature stated in recipe until firm. Round cake will take about 30-35 minutes, rectangular cake will take about 35-45 minutes.

To assemble

Cut Morgan's body template (see page 74) and Teddy's head template (see page 75) and pin to cakes as shown in **Step 1**.

STEP 1

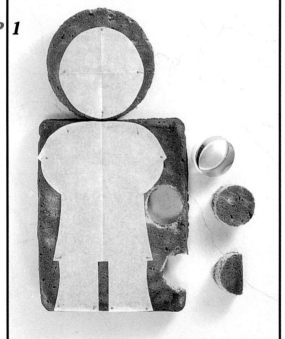

Cut to shape. Using a 6 cm round cutter, cut a circle and semicircle from remaining rectangular cake. Trim circle to a dome shape for snout. Split semicircle in halves horizontally

to form two hands and cut two small 'v's in each to indicate fingers. Using the same 6 cm round cutter, cut two ear shapes from remaining round cake as shown in **Step 2**. Scoop out a small hollow in each.

STEP 2

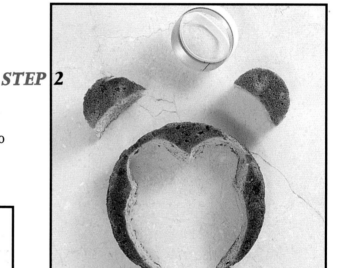

Place Morgan on a 30 cm x 60 cm cake board as shown in **Step 3**, leaving hands aside.

STEP 3

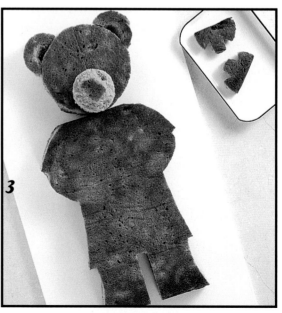

To decorate

Colour ½ cup frosting green. Colour half the remaining frosting with a mixture of caramel and orange food colouring. Colour remaining half violet. Spread frosting over cake as shown in **Step 4**.

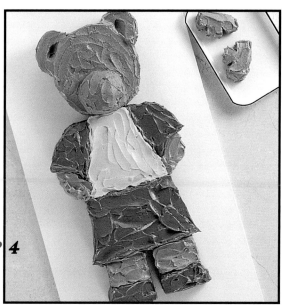

STEP 4

Mark line for pants with a knife. Roll 60 g white soft icing into a 1 cm thick circle (see directions for rolling soft icing page 8). Cut with the 6 cm round cutter. Cut in half to form two semicircles and place on cake for shoe toes. Trim lime milk bottles and place on top of shoes to form bows. Place peppermints above bows for shoe tongues, and strips of lime candy fruit sticks for laces. Set 'Happy Birthday' banner at Morgan's waist. Knead violet food colouring into remaining 30 g white soft icing and roll into a square shape, 4 cm x 4 cm. Refrigerate

for 30 minutes. Trim edges square then place on Morgan's shirt. Cut musk sticks to form 'M's and place on sleeves, pants and in centre of Morgan's violet square. Place trimmed liquorice in position for mouth. Place a hand on each side of 'Happy Birthday' banner as shown in final picture.

The young helper can . . .

- Trim Morgan's shirt collar with a lime candy fruit stick and position the two dark brown Smarties on his face for eyes. Finish off with the large black jellybean for nose.

Notes

- *A 6 cm round template (see page 75) can be used instead of cutter.*

- *Gift box plaque (see page 9) may be used in place of 'Happy Birthday' banner.*

- *A small chocolate egg may be used for Morgan's nose in place of a large black jelly bean.*

Amy

YOU WILL NEED

2 quantities cake mixture
(see recipes page 5)

1½ quantities frosting
(see recipe page 7)

caramel and blue food colourings

60 g pre-packaged white soft icing

8 strawberry milk bottle sweets
for bows

2 large round peppermints
for shoe tongues

9 musk sticks for shoes,
shirt and skirt trims

gift box plaque
(see page 9)

Smarties for eyes and shirt badge

1 large black jelly bean for nose

liquorice stick for mouth

jelly beans for skirt pattern

To bake

Pour 2 cups cake mixture into a greased and lined 17 cm round cake pan. Pour remaining cake mixture into a similarly prepared 25 cm x 30 cm lamington pan. Bake at temperature stated in recipe until firm. Round cake will take about 30-35 minutes, rectangular cake will take about 35-45 minutes.

To assemble

Cut Amy's body template (see page 74) and Teddy's head template (see page 75) and pin to cakes as shown in **Step 1**.

STEP **1**

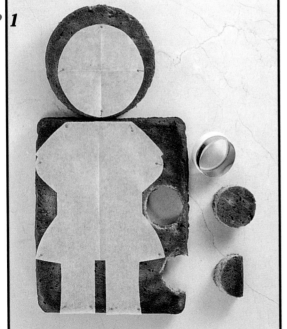

Cut to shape. Using a 6 cm round cutter, cut a circle and a semicircle from remaining rectangular cake. Trim circle to a dome shape for snout. Split semicircle in halves horizontally

to form two hands. Cut two small 'v's in each to indicate fingers. Using the 6 cm cutter, cut two ear shapes from remaining round cake as shown in **Step 2**. Scoop out a small hollow in each.

STEP **2**

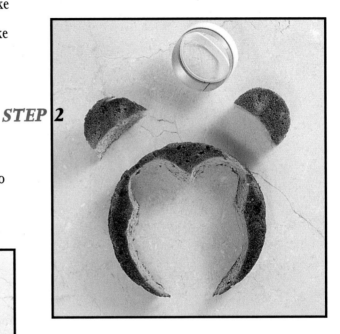

Place Amy on a 30 cm x 60 cm cake board as shown in **Step 3**, leaving hands aside.

STEP **3**

To decorate

Reserve ⅓ cup uncoloured frosting. Colour half the remaining frosting beige using caramel food colouring, and the other half blue. Spread frosting over cake as shown in **Step 4**.

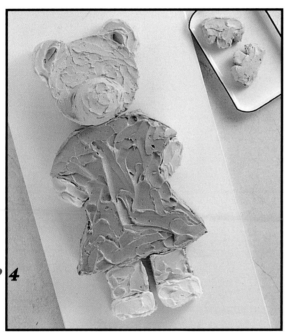

STEP 4

Roll white soft icing into a 1 cm thick circle (see directions for rolling soft icing page 8). Cut with the 6 cm round cutter. Cut in half to form two semicircles and place on cake for shoe toes. Trim four strawberry milk bottles and place on top of shoes to form bows. Place peppermints above bows for shoe tongues and strips of musk stick for laces. Place 3 musk sticks on a baking tray lined with non-stick baking paper and bake at 180°C for 20-30 seconds, until pliable. Gently bend into waves and when cool use to decorate hem of Amy's

skirt. Trim remaining milk bottles and place on Amy's head for bows. Position the Smarties for eyes, black jellybean for nose, and trimmed liquorice for mouth. Set gift box plaque at Amy's waist and place a hand on each side as shown in final picture.

The young helper can . . .

- Finish the musk stick trim on Amy's shirt, place the Smartie badge in the centre and scatter the jellybeans over her skirt.

Notes

- *A 6 cm round template (see page 75) can be used instead of cutter.*

- *'Happy Birthday' banner (see page 9) can be used in place of gift box plaque.*

- *A small chocolate egg may be used for Amy's nose instead of the large black jellybean.*

Johnson

YOU WILL NEED

2 quantities cake mixture
(see recipes page 5)

1 x 250 g pre-packaged Swiss roll

4 pre-packaged jam sponge rollettes

1½ quantities frosting
(see recipe page 7)

black and pink food colourings

1 white marshmallow for *eyes*

2 dark brown Smarties for *eyes*

To bake

Pour 2 cups cake mixture into a greased and
lined 17 cm round cake pan. Pour remaining
cake mixture into a similarly prepared
25 cm x 30 cm lamington pan. Bake at
temperature stated in recipe until firm. Round
cake, about 30-35 minutes, rectangular cake,
about 35-45 minutes.

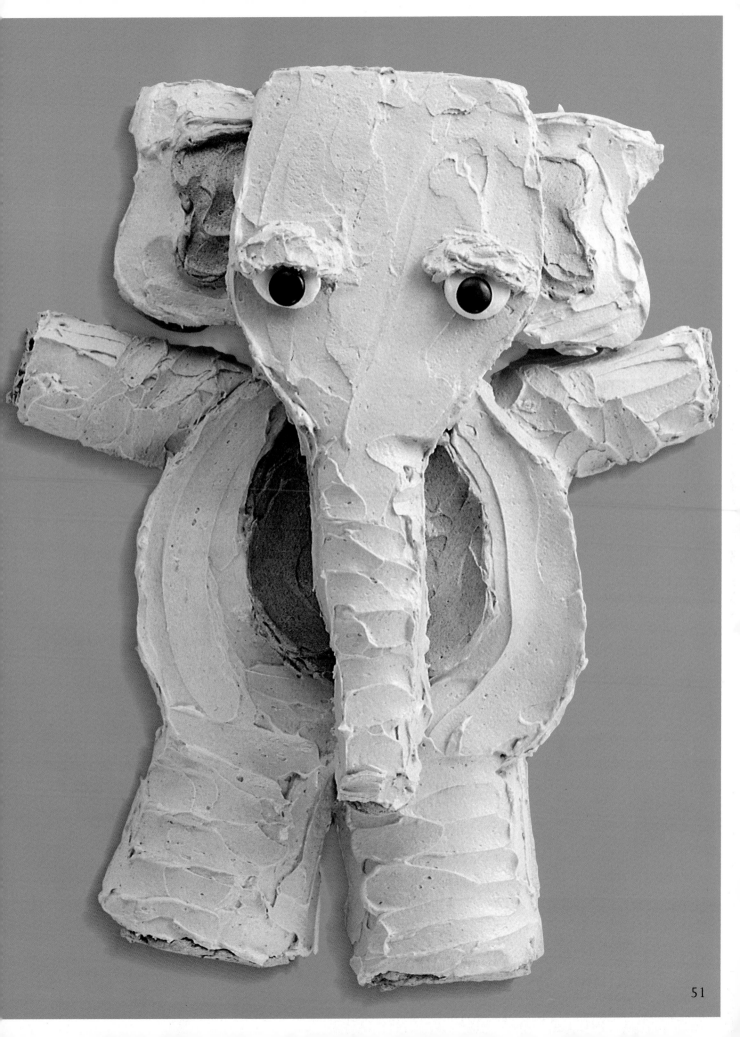

To assemble

Cut Johnson's templates (see page 76) and pin to cakes as shown in **Step 1**.

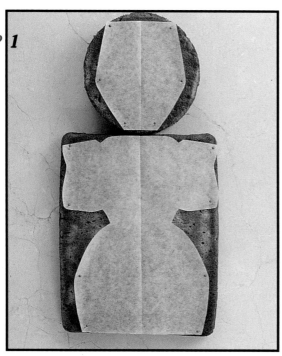

STEP **1**

Cut to shape. Place large cake shape on a 35 cm x 45 cm cake board, leaving smaller one aside. Cut Swiss roll in half lengthwise. Cut one half into two pieces for legs. Place into position

STEP **2**

on cake board. Trim two of the rollettes for trunk, and the remaining two for arms, and set aside as shown in **Step 2**.

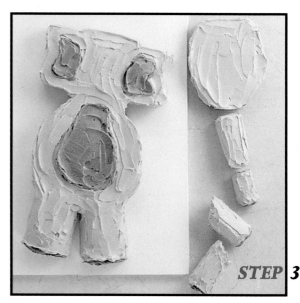

STEP **3**

To decorate

Colour 1 cup frosting grey. Colour remaining frosting pink. Spread pink frosting over face, trunk, arms and body, leaving inside of ears, stomach, ends of legs, arms and trunk unfrosted. Spread grey frosting on bare patches as shown in **Step 3**.

Place face, trunk and arms in position. Smooth over joints with pink frosting and make wrinkles in legs and trunk with a small spatula or butter knife. Using scissors, cut two slices of the marshmallow for eyes. Place in position, sticky sides facing up.

The young helper can . . .

- Top each eye with a Smartie, then the cook can spread a little pink frosting over the top of each eye for eyelids.

McDuff

53

McDuff

small quantity biscuit dough
(see recipe page 6)

2 quantities cake mixture
(see recipes page 5)

1 quantity frosting (see recipe page 7)

blue, yellow and red food colourings

yellow candy fruit sticks

30 g pre-packaged white soft icing

liquorice stick

To bake

Roll biscuit dough out to 1 cm thickness (see directions for rolling biscuit dough with recipe page 6). Cut McDuff's face template (see page 76) and place on biscuit dough as shown in **Step 1**. Cut dough to shape. Lift paper base and face shape onto a baking tray. Bake at 170° C for 30 - 40 minutes, until golden brown.

Pour cake mixture evenly into two greased and lined 23 cm square slab pans. Bake at temperature stated in recipe until firm, about 25-35 minutes.

McDuff

STEP 1

To decorate

Colour ½ cup frosting blue and colour remaining frosting yellow. As shown in **Step 4**, spread yellow and ⅓ of blue frosting over cake. Spread remaining blue frosting over biscuit face. Position face on top of yellow frosting. Cut yellow candy fruit sticks and place on cake as shown in final picture. Roll two small balls of white soft icing (about the size of shelled hazelnuts). Flatten and place on McDuff's face for eyes. Colour remaining soft icing red for mouth and form into an 11 cm long sausage shape. Roll into a rectangular shape 1.5 cm wide x 13 cm long (see directions for rolling soft icing page 8). Refrigerate 30 minutes and trim edges. Position on face.

STEP 2

STEP 3

The young helper can . . .

- Top each eye with a slice of liquorice and place a piece of liquorice in the centre of face for nose. Place two slices of yellow candy fruit stick on mouth.

STEP 4

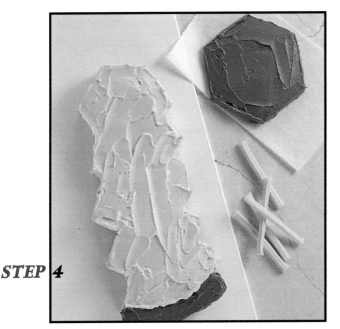

Notes

- *Should you only have one 23 cm square slab pan, prepare and bake the cakes one at a time.*
- *Dough off-cuts can be shaped into small cookies and baked.*
- *Unfrosted biscuit face can be made up to a week in advance and stored in an airtight container.*

To assemble

Cut McDuff's body template (see page 76) and pin to cakes as shown in **Step 2**. Cut to shape. Place shapes on a 25 cm x 45 cm cake board as shown in **Step 3**.

Squeaky

YOU WILL NEED

1 quantity banana cake mixture
(see recipe page 5)
or 1 x 340 g packet butter cake mixture
(made as directed on packet)

1 quantity frosting (see recipe page 7)

1 Wagon Wheel for neck plates

2 x twin peaks of Toblerone
(from a 100 g bar) for pincers

black and red food colourings

aniseed jelly rings for neck, hat, eyes, and wheels

silver cachous for silver bands

2 maraschino cherries for eyes

orange candy fruit sticks for trim
around eyes and for grates

flat liquorice strap for arm trim

2 icing bandaids (see recipe page 10)

1 jube for light

2 red pipe cleaners

1 metal skewer

To bake

Pour cake mixture into a greased and lined
25 cm x 30 cm lamington pan. Bake at
temperature stated in recipe until firm, about
30-40 minutes.

To assemble

Colour ¼ cup frosting red. Colour remaining frosting dark grey.

Cut Squeaky's body template (see page 77) and pin to cake, as shown in **Step 1**. Cut to shape. Using an 8 cm round cutter, cut a circle from remaining cake.

As shown in **Step 2** position large cake shape on a 35 cm x 40cm cake board. Cut Wagon Wheel in half and position one half as Squeaky's lower neck plate. Set other half aside. Trim Toblerone peaks to sit evenly on board and postion at end of each arm to form pincers.

Cut cake circle in half to form two semicircles. Sandwich together with a little dark grey frosting and trim to the shape of Squeaky's head. Set aside.

STEP **1**

STEP **2**

STEP **3**

To decorate

Spread dark grey frosting over lower neck plate and body, leaving arms and pincers bare. Place an aniseed jelly ring on top of frosted neck plate. Cover head with dark grey frosting. Cover other half of Wagon Wheel with dark grey frosting and place into position on top of aniseed jelly ring as shown in **Step 3**. Use an egg slice to lift head into position. Spread red frosting over arms and pincers.

Using a skewer, mark guide lines in frosting where silver cachous will lay. Place cachous along lines using tweezers.

Press a maraschino cherry into the centre of an aniseed jelly ring. Place into eye position. Repeat for other eye. Rim each eye with a thin slice of orange candy fruit stick.

Form two grate patterns with orange candy fruit sticks. Place pieces of flat liquorice strap on each arm. Cut an aniseed jelly ring in half and use for wheels. Position bandaids, twisted red pipe cleaners and metal skewer as shown in final picture.

The young helper can . . .

- Place jube light between grates and an aniseed jelly ring on top of Squeaky's head.

Note

- *An 8 cm round template (see page 75) can be used instead of cutter.*

Alfred

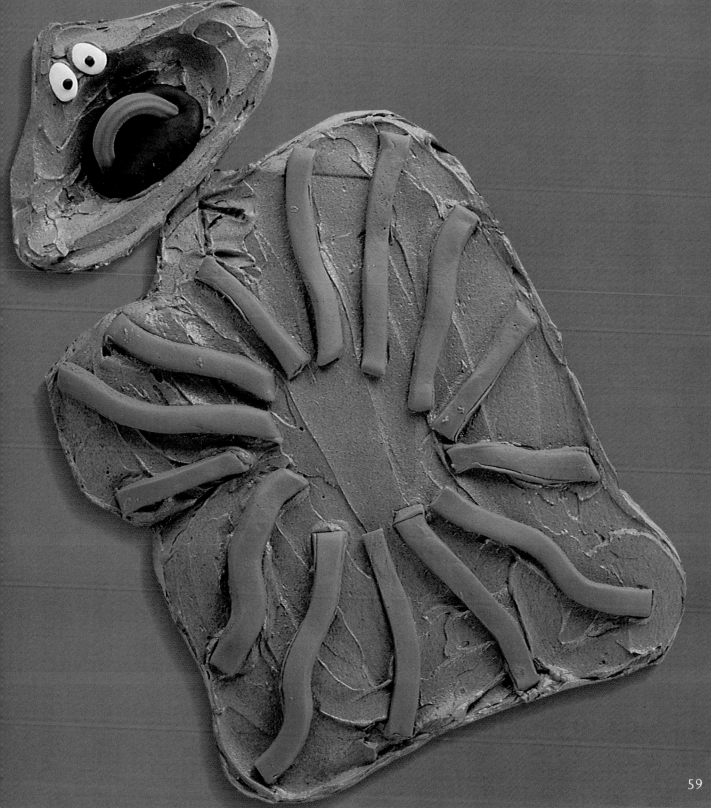

Alfred

YOU WILL NEED

2 quantities cake mixture
(see recipes page 5)

green and black food colourings

1 quantity frosting
(see recipe page 7)

175 g pre-packaged white soft icing

1 musk stick for *plug*

To bake

Pour 2 cups cake mixture into a greased and lined 17 cm round cake pan. Pour remaining cake mixture into a similarly prepared 25 cm x 30 cm lamington pan. Bake at temperature stated in recipe until firm. Round cake will take about 30-35 minutes, rectangular cake will take about 35-45 minutes.

Alfred

To assemble

Cut Alfred's templates (see page 73) and pin to cakes as shown in **Step 1.** Cut to shape.

Hollow out smaller cake using a grapefruit knife or small sharp knife as shown in **Step 2.** Place cakes on a 35 cm x 45 cm cake board as shown in **Step 3.**

To decorate

Colour frosting green and spread over entire cake. Colour 150 g white soft icing green. Roll out into a rectangular shape 10 cm x 14 cm, about 5mm thick (see directions for rolling icing page 8) and refrigerate 1 hour. Trim edges of rectangle and cut into fourteen strips (1 cm wide) in lengths varying from 5 cm - 10 cm as shown in **Step 4.**

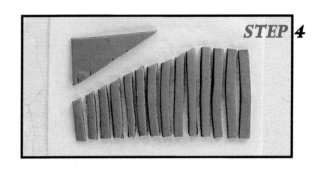

Bend strips into position on cake as shown in final picture. From remaining 25 g white soft icing, take two pea size pieces, form into egg shapes and flatten for eyes. Colour remaining white soft icing black. For eyeballs, form two very tiny pieces of black icing into balls. Shape remaining black icing into a ball and flatten slightly. Cut musk stick to 7 cm in length, place on a baking tray lined with non-stick baking paper and bake at 180°C for 20-30 seconds, until pliable. Gently curve and place on black plug. Position on cake. Using a sharp knife, mark an 'A' at Alfred's neck as shown in final picture.

The young helper can . . .

- Lick the beaters!

Mr Squiggle

YOU WILL NEED

1 quantity cake mixture
(see recipe page 5)

1 x 250 g pre-packaged Swiss roll

4 pre-packaged jam sponge rollettes

1½ quantities frosting (see recipe page 7)

caramel, green, red and black food colourings

1 small round biscuit

200 g pre-packaged white soft icing
for *pencil detail and eye*

1 flat liquorice strap for *detailing*

liquorice stick for *detailing*

1 pink marshmallow for *cheek*

1 large white marshmallow
for *hat pompom*

red satin ribbon for *bow*

Mr Squiggle

To bake

Pour cake mixture into a greased and lined 23 cm square slab pan. Bake at temperature stated in recipe until firm, about 35-45 minutes.

To assemble

Cut Mr Squiggle's head template (see page 78) and pin to cake as shown in **Step 1**. Cut to shape. Cut collar shape from remaining cake.

STEP 2

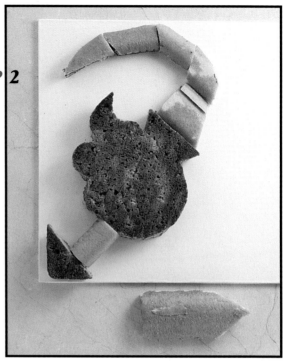

STEP 1

As shown in **Step 2**, position large cake shape on a 43 cm x 43 cm cake board. Cut Swiss roll in half lengthwise. Trim one half to a point and set aside for nose. Trim remaining half and three jam rollettes to form hat. Position remaining jam rollette for neck and cake off-cut for collar.

To decorate

Leave 1 cup frosting uncoloured. Colour 2 tablespoons frosting dark grey and reserve for squiggle on cakeboard. Colour half remaining frosting green and reserve 1 teaspoon for eyeshadow. Colour other half beige using caramel colouring. Spread uncoloured frosting over nose, collar and cap trim. Spread green frosting over hair and cap. Cover face, neck and biscuit with beige frosting and place biscuit into position for ear as shown in **Step 3**.

Colour 175 g white soft icing red. Roll out to a rectangular shape 13 cm x 14 cm, about 5 mm thick (see directions for rolling soft icing page 8). Refrigerate one hour. Cut Mr Squiggle nose template (see page 78) and place on top of soft icing. Cut to shape as shown in **Step 4**.

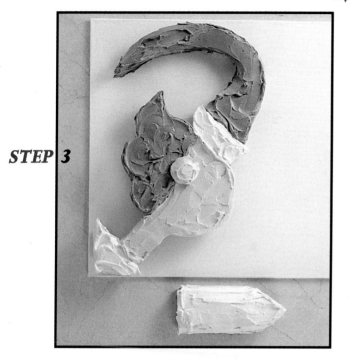

STEP 3

Roll remaining white soft icing to 5 mm thickness. Cut into a 5 cm long oval shape for eye and set into position. Mark eyelid with a fine strip of flat liquorice strap and spread reserved green frosting over eyelid. Decorate nose and hat with strips of flat liquorice strap. Cut pieces of liquorice stick for mouth, eye details, freckles and pencil point. Cut a slice of pink marshmallow for cheek.

STEP 4

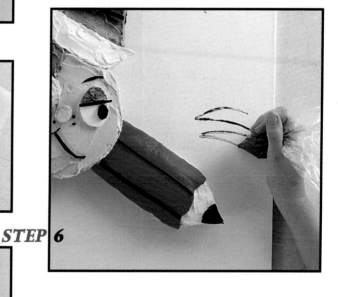

STEP 6

STEP 5

Leaving template against icing, turn over and peel away top paper. Use template to help position icing on top of nose as shown in **Step 5**. Peel away template. Place nose into position using an egg slice.

Place dark grey icing in an oven bag. Snip a small hole in one corner. Hold close to cake board and pipe out a squiggle as shown in **Step 6**.

The young helper can . . .

- Place the large white marshmallow at the end of cap for pom pom and position bow.

Princess Raggy Doll

YOU WILL NEED

2 quantities cake mixture
(see recipes page 5)

1 'Happy Birthday' banner (see page 9)
keeping icing off-cuts for *nose and eyes*

1 quantity frosting (see recipe page 7)

blue, yellow, pink and
caramel food colourings

liquorice stick for *eyes and mouth*

2 pink Smarties for *cheeks*

yellow, orange and green candy fruit sticks
for *hair, shirt and skirt stripes*

liquorice allsorts for *checks*

small round white sweets for *skirt polkadots*

To bake

Pour 2 cups cake mixture into a greased and
lined 17 cm round cake pan. Pour remaining
cake mixture into a similarly prepared
25 cm x 30 cm lamington pan. Bake at
temperature stated in recipe until firm. Round
cake will take about 30-35 minutes, rectangular
cake will take about 35-45 minutes.

Note

A 6cm round template may
be used instead of cutter
(see page 75).

Princess Raggy Doll

To assemble

Cut Princess Raggy Doll's templates (see page 72) and pin to cakes, as shown in **Step 1**.

Using a 6 cm round cutter, cut a circle from remaining rectangular cake. Trim circle to 1.5 cm thick and cut in half to form two semicircles. Trim each to an oval shape for hands. As shown in **Step 2**, place cakes into position on a 25 cm x 45 cm cake board, leaving hands aside. Using a small piece of soft icing from 'Happy Birthday' banner off-cuts, form an oval shape for nose.

STEP 2   STEP 3

STEP 1

To decorate

Reserve ½ cup uncoloured frosting. Colour ½ cup yellow, colour ¼ cup blue, colour 2 tablespoons pink, and colour remaining frosting skin tone using a mixture of pink and caramel colourings. As shown in **Step 3**, spread frosting over cake and hands. Cover nose with skin tone frosting and set into place. Form two soft icing off-cuts (the size of shelled hazelnuts) into egg shapes and flatten into ovals. Colour another small soft icing off-cut blue. Form into two pea size balls,

flatten into circles and place on top of ovals. Place in eye position on face and top each with a very small piece of liquorice. Cut a slice of liquorice into mouth shape and place into position. Place two pink Smarties on face for cheeks. Cut yellow and orange candy fruit sticks and piece together on yellow frosting for hair.

Cut one orange and two yellow candy fruit sticks into 4 cm lengths and taper each into a point at one end. Gently push tapered end into cake at back of head for the three upstanding hair strands. Set 'Happy Birthday' banner at waist. Cut pieces of orange candy fruit sticks and piece together to form shirt. Slice green candy fruit sticks into thin strips and place on white portion of skirt. Slice white part of liquorice allsorts into squares and place on blue portions of skirt to form checks. Use lengths of orange candy fruit sticks for stockings. Place hands into position as shown in final picture.

The young helper can . . .

- Place round white sweets on yellow panels of skirt for polkadots.

68

Templates

Templates

Fold along this line

Princess Raggy Doll's body

B1 and B

Fold a

Templates are used as a guide when cutting. These templates are the correct size for the cakes you will make. Simply trace them onto non-stick baking paper with a felt tip pen.

Symmetrical Templates

Fold a sheet of non-stick baking paper, large enough for the whole template, in half and place over the half template you require, lining up the fold line of the paper with the fold line indicated on the template. Trace template, cut out and unfold the paper.

Circular Templates

Fold a sheet of non-stick baking paper large enough for the whole circle in quarters. Place over the quarter circle template you require, lining up the fold lines of paper with the fold lines indicated in the book. Trace, cut out and unfold the paper.

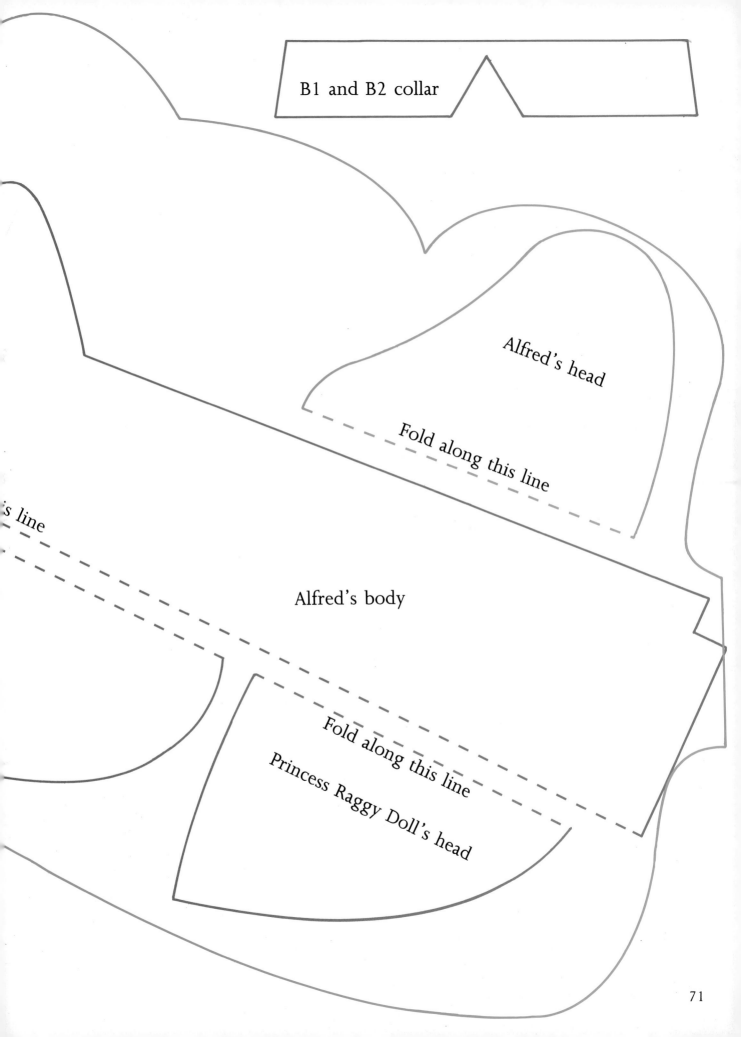

B1 and B2 collar

Alfred's head

Fold along this line

's line

Alfred's body

Fold along this line

Princess Raggy Doll's head

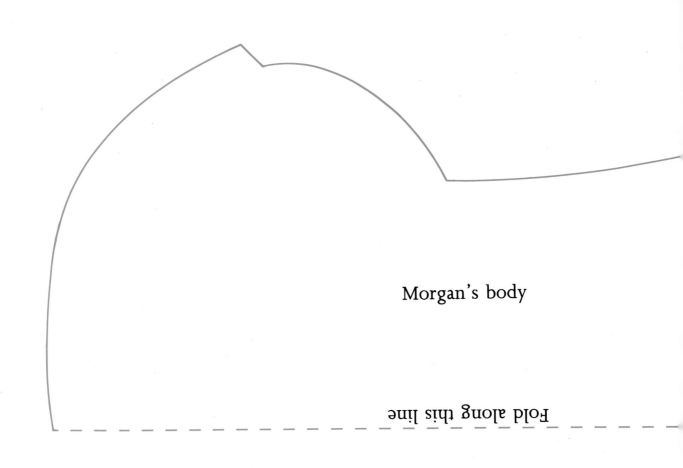

Morgan's body

Fold along this line

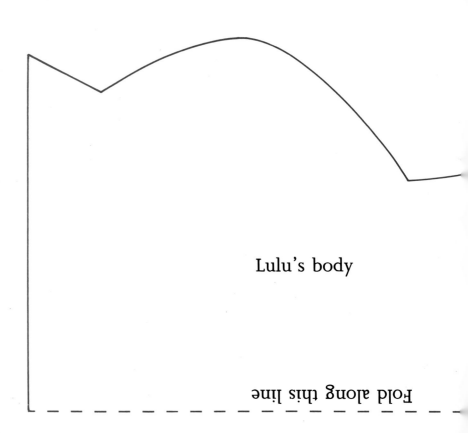

Lulu's body

Fold along this line

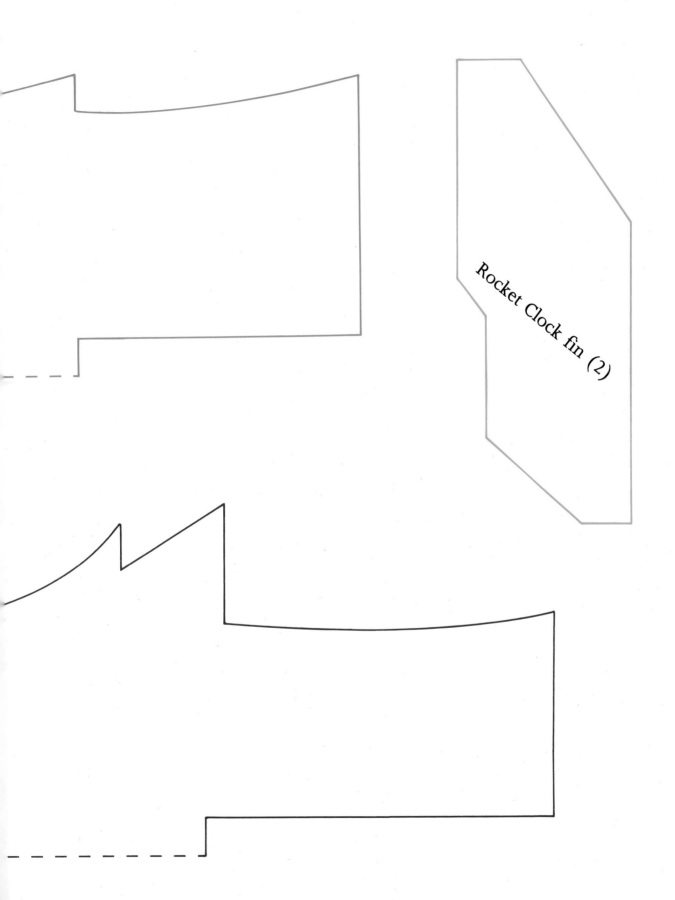

Rocket Clock fin (2)

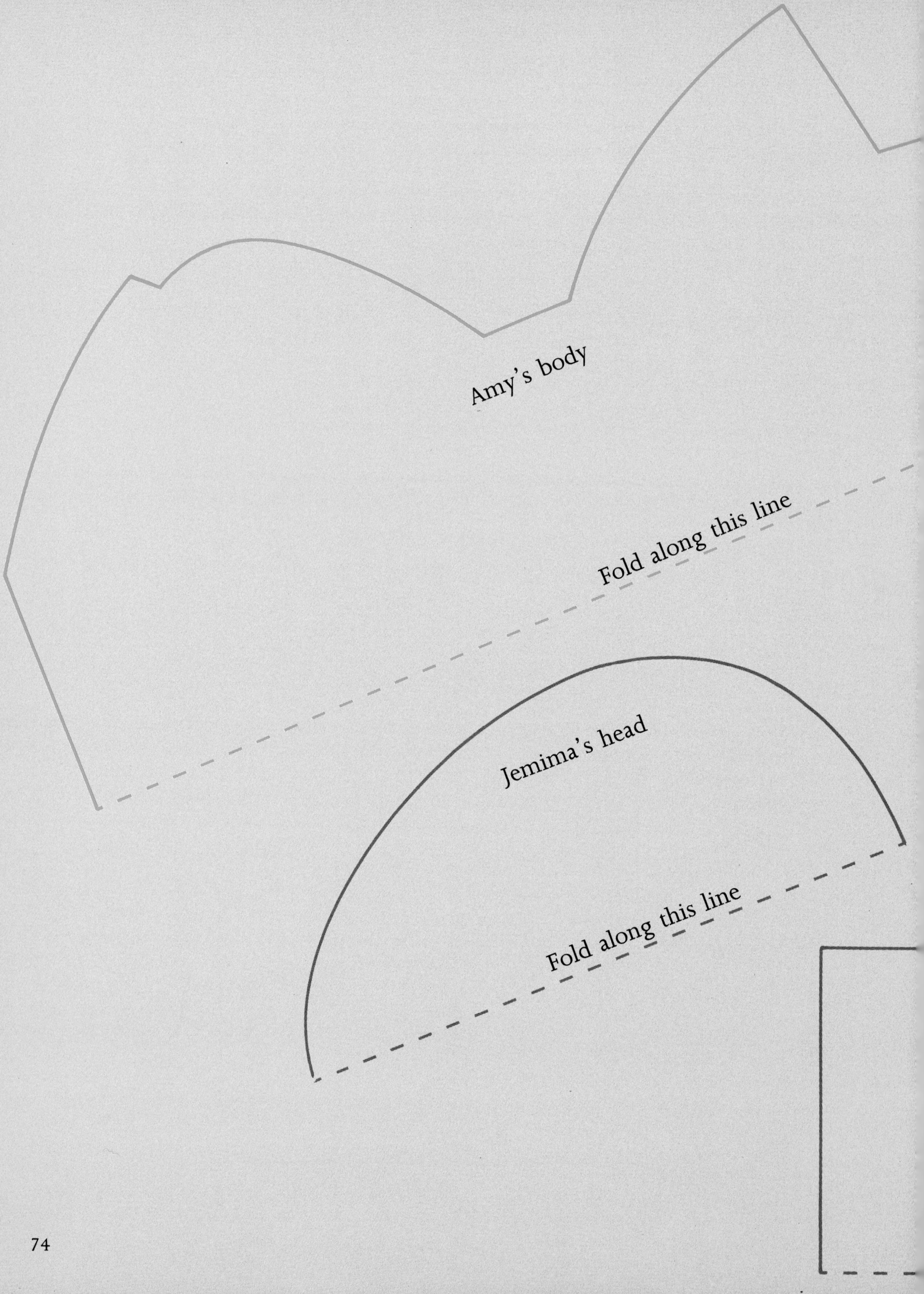

Amy's body

Fold along this line

Jemima's head

Fold along this line

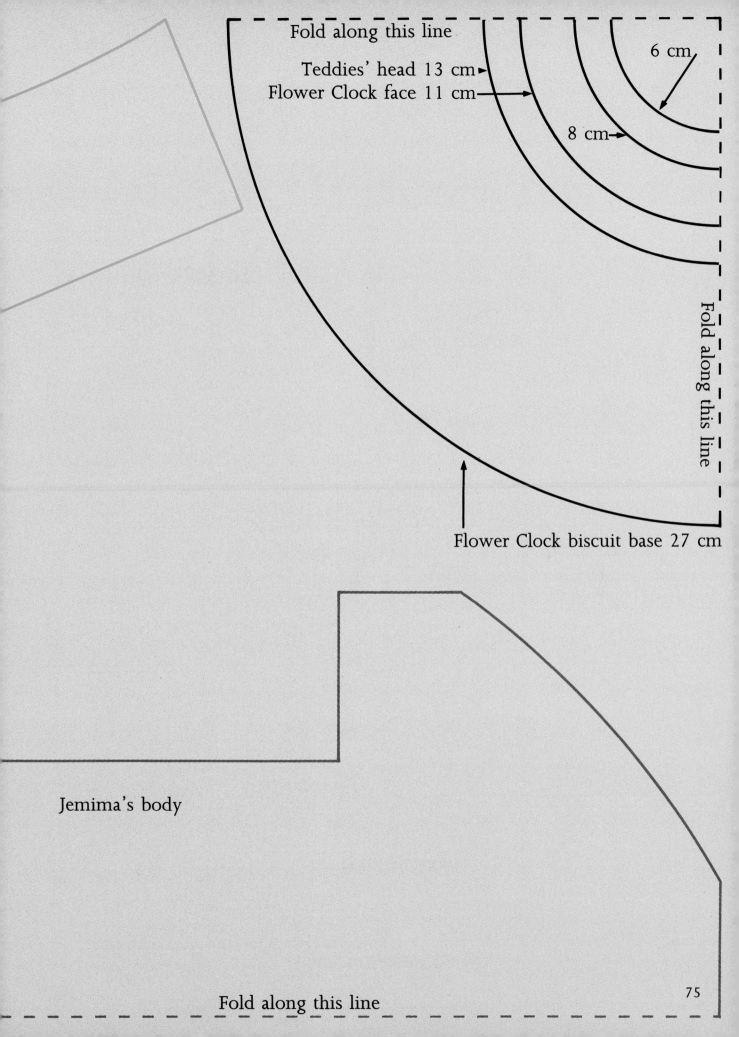

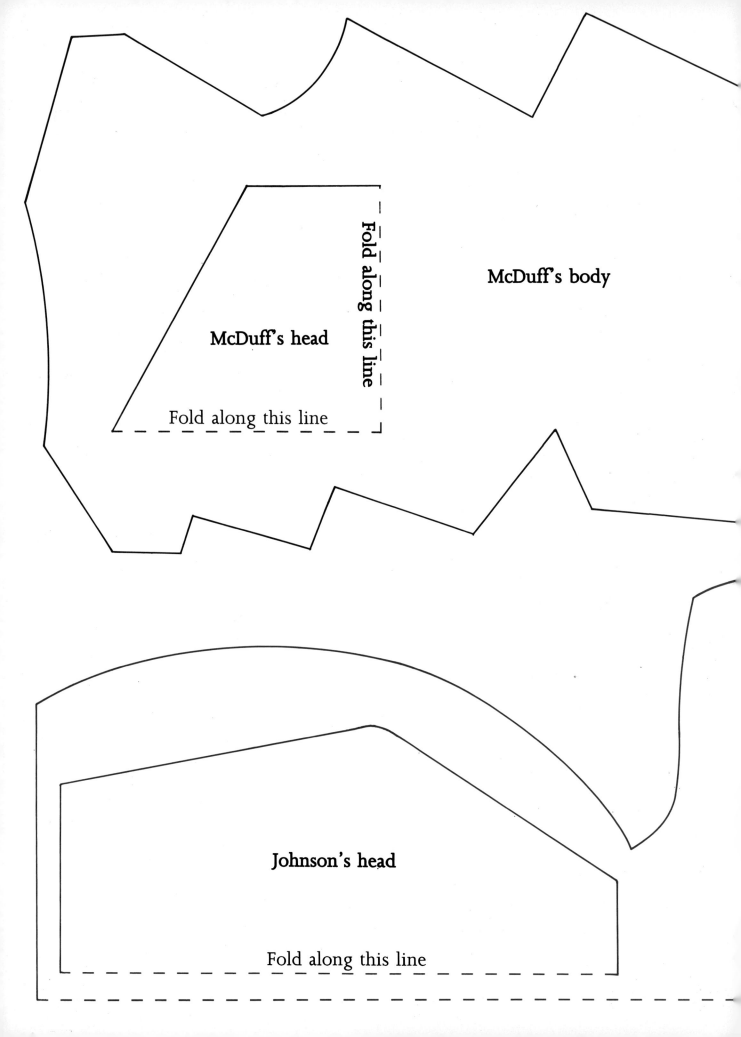

McDuff's body

Fold along this line

McDuff's head

Fold along this line

Johnson's head

Fold along this line

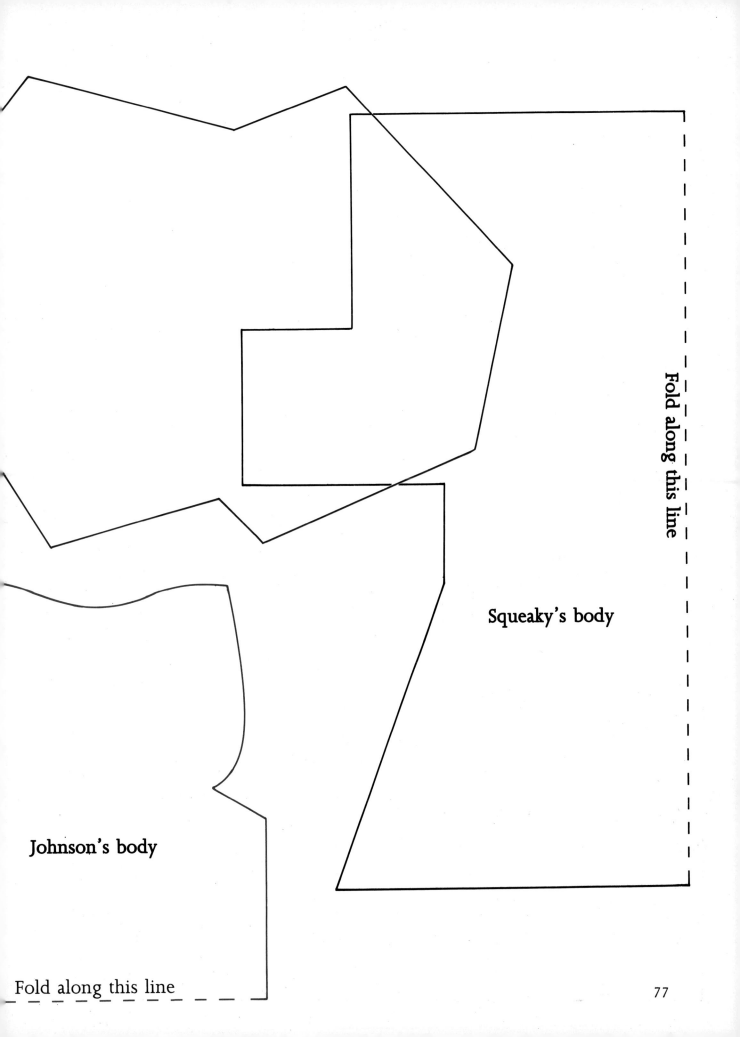

Squeaky's body

Johnson's body

Fold along this line

Fold along this line

77

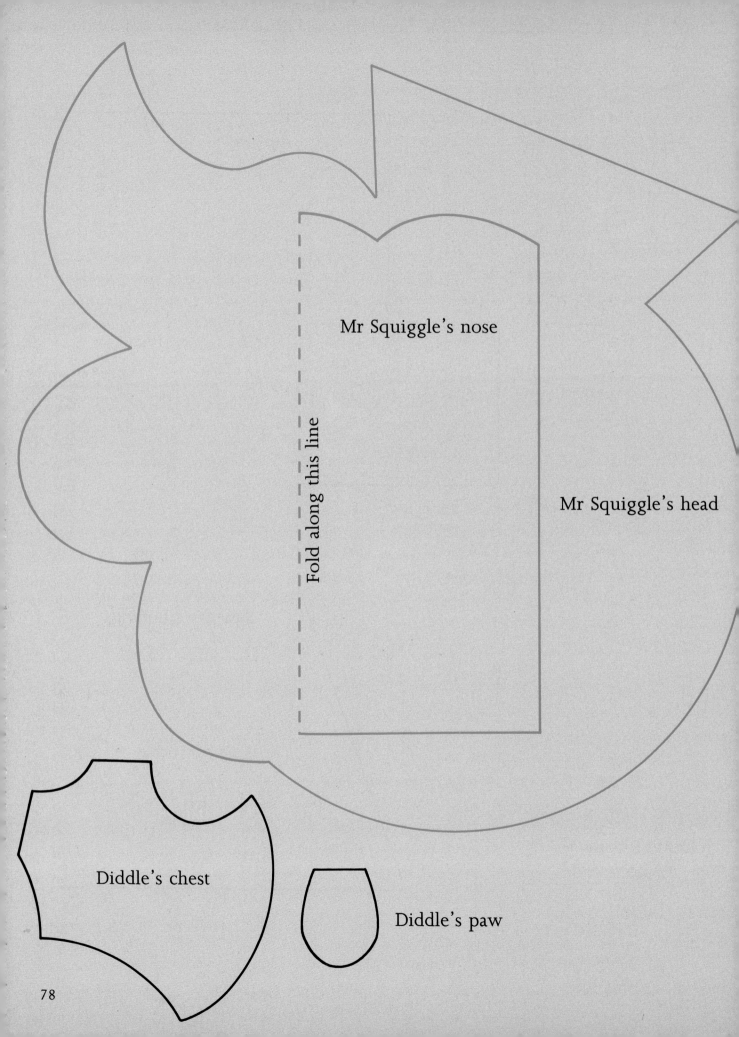

Mr Squiggle's nose

Mr Squiggle's head

Fold along this line

Diddle's chest

Diddle's paw